TAYLOR-MADE TALES

THE PIRATE'S PLOT

This Book Belongs to

connor

TAYLOR-MADE TALES

THE PIRATE'S PLOT

by

ELLEN MILES

AN
APPLE
PAPERBACK

SCHOLASTIC INC.
New York   London   Toronto   Auckland   Sydney
Mexico City   Hong Kong   New Delhi   Buenos Aires

ISBN 0-439-59709-9

12 11 10 9 8 7 6 5 4 3 2 1   6 7 8 9 10 11/0

Printed in the U.S.A.   40

First printing, June 2006

For W.R., who is nothing like his
traitorous namesake!

Leo Calls It Quits

I'm quitting soccer!"

Leo blurted it out without even waiting for Mr. Taylor to say, "Good morning, class! Who has something to share?"

That was how sharing time usually started in room 3B, at least since Mr. Taylor had been their teacher — which wasn't very long. In fact, he was so new that Leo was still kind of trying to figure him out.

Tall, skinny Mr. Taylor was not like any other teacher Leo had met.

For one thing, Mr. Taylor told stories — the best stories Leo had ever heard! And he made them up out of nothing. Well, not exactly nothing. Mr. Taylor could take any five things — any five things in the universe! — and tell about them all in a story. Taylor-Made Tales, he called them. He had a big red notebook on his desk, with that name written upon it in gold letters. It was full of stories he had made up.

Mr. Taylor was also different from other teachers because he never got upset about little things like people not raising their hands. He seemed to understand that kids got excited sometimes and just had to burst out with whatever it was they had to tell — right that second.

Usually during sharing time Leo told a joke. He was known for it. "Leo's joke of the day," his friend Cricket called it. But today he didn't feel like joking.

He felt angry.

He felt like quitting soccer.

Leo was crazy about soccer. He had been playing since he was about four years old. He was good, too! It was as if his feet knew what to do. He didn't have to look at the ball at all as he dribbled it all the way up the field and aimed it perfectly at the goal.

But he had been thinking about quitting soccer all morning, ever since he woke up and saw his shin guards sitting by his soccer bag. There was practice today and a game tomorrow, and for the first time in his life Leo did not feel like playing soccer.

Leo looked at Mr. Taylor, waiting to see what he would say.

Mr. Taylor didn't say anything at first. He just nodded. He frowned a little, and his bushy eyebrows frowned, too. "Really?" he asked calmly. "I thought you liked soccer." He leaned forward in the big green chair that was in the reading corner, where they always had sharing time. The reading corner was filled with brightly colored pillows. Leo had grabbed his favorite pillow, the one shaped like a huge purple frog.

"Wait," Mr. Taylor said. "Don't tell me. Let me guess. Is it because you're tired of all the running around? I know how you hate that."

Everybody laughed. Leo's friend Cricket laughed hardest of all. Leo glared at her. He knew Mr. Taylor was just teasing, but still, Leo didn't like being laughed at. The thing was, Leo loved to run, and everybody knew it. Most days he ran all the way to school, getting there early so he could play kickball and run around in the playground before the bell rang. He was always the first one out of the room at recess. And after he ran home, he usually spent an hour or so running around in his backyard with his dog, Tracker.

Leo crossed his arms over his chest. "No," he said flatly. "It's not because of that."

Mr. Taylor raised an eyebrow, as if he were saying, "Well?"

Leo groaned. "We have a new coach this year, and soccer's no fun anymore," he said. "It's all the stupid drills."

"Go on," said Mr. Taylor. He was nodding and listening carefully. Leo liked the way Mr. Taylor knew when to take things seriously.

"Does Leo get to talk for the whole meeting?" Jennifer interrupted, tossing her hair. Jennifer was always tossing her hair. She was blond, like her twin brother, Jason, and practically every day she came to school with a new hairdo. Today she had her hair in pigtails, with purple ties on the ends.

Leo felt like yanking on one of those dumb pig-tails. "I just got started!" he said. "Anyway, you talked for about an hour yesterday about your new kitten."

Mr. Taylor held up a hand. "Hold on," he said. "Remind me. How do we treat one another in this classroom?"

Everybody said it at the same time. "With respect!" they shouted back.

The teacher smiled. "Good," he said. "Just wanted to make sure we all remembered."

Jennifer looked as if she wanted to roll her eyes, but she didn't.

Mr. Taylor nodded at Leo. "So?" he asked. "What about your coach?"

Leo sighed. "He thinks he knows everything. Like, he's the only one who knows the best way to learn soccer. I mean, my uncle Jim knows more than he does. Uncle Jim's the one who taught me how to head a ball. And Coach Hauser doesn't even let us do that. He says we're too young for heading," Leo said. "It's just rules, rules, rules and drills, drills, drills. Soccer's no fun anymore."

"Hmm," said Mr. Taylor. "Quitting soccer would be a pretty big decision, wouldn't it?"

Leo nodded.

"My mother always used to tell me to sleep on it before I decided something like that," said Mr. Taylor.

Leo pictured a soccer ball under his pillow. He smiled for the first time all morning.

Mr. Taylor smiled back. "That's better," he said. "Meanwhile, how about if we start a new Taylor-Made Tale to give you something else to think about?"

"Yeah!" everybody yelled. Even Molly, the quietest, shyest girl in third grade.

"Who gets to choose what's in it?" asked Oliver.

All the kids had been keeping lists. If they got called on, they wanted to be ready. What five items would make the best story?

"Leo does," said Mr. Taylor.

Leo lit up. "Really?" he asked.

"Hey!" yelled Jason.

"Why Leo?" asked Jennifer.

"What about me?" Oliver asked.

"You'll all get a turn," said Mr. Taylor, holding up his hands. "But today is Leo's turn."

There was something in his voice that made it clear there was no point in arguing. Everybody turned to look at Leo.

"So?" Mr. Taylor asked Leo. "Do you have a list?"

Leo had been waiting for this moment. He had been thinking a lot about what items he would like to have in his very own Taylor-Made Tale. "I want my story to be about something that could really happen," he said. "No talking dogs or anything like that." He had loved the last story, about a dog who had learned to talk, but he knew it was made up. No dog could really speak English!

"No talking dogs," said Mr. Taylor, smiling. "Check."

"But I want it to be exciting, too," Leo went on. "So I want it to have a pirate ship in it."

Oliver cheered. He loved ships of any kind.

Leo went on with his list. "And a six-toed cat, and a big chunk of cheese, and a brass key . . ." He had tried to pick things that had no connection at all to each other. It was kind of a test for Mr. Taylor. Could he make an exciting story out of a bunch of random items?

But Leo suddenly remembered that he had only thought of four items so far. He needed one more. He looked around the classroom, thinking hard.

Boy, Mr. Taylor had really changed the way room 3B looked. He'd created the reading corner with all the comfy cushions, changed around the computer area, and added lots of bookshelves. But the coolest change was that he had started to bring in his collection of interesting things — curios, he called them.

They were arranged throughout the classroom: on the windowsills, on Mr. Taylor's desk, and even next to the sink in the cleanup area. Mr. Taylor brought in something new every Wednesday and told the class all about what it was and where it came from. There were a fan from Japan; a huge stone coin from some island in the South Seas; a pair of gold-embroidered red felt slippers from Lapland, where the reindeer live; and a tiny hummingbird's nest from Brazil. Mr. Taylor had all sorts of amazing things!

But Leo didn't want any of those things in his tale. He wanted to make sure his was a real story about real things that could happen to real people. He kept looking around the room.

"And . . . a mop!" he said when he spotted one standing in the corner near the door. There. That was a nice, ordinary item. Now the story would have to be real. "I want a mop in my story." Leo waited, wondering if Mr. Taylor would tell him to choose something else. Maybe his items were *too* random. How could they all be in the same story? Maybe Mr. Taylor would have to think about it overnight. Maybe he wouldn't be able to do it!

But Mr. Taylor didn't even blink. "Uh-huh!" he said, nodding. "Well, that would be the one about the time Tom stowed away on Captain Blaine's ship. Perfect!" He sat back in his chair and closed his eyes for a moment. His chest rose and fell as he took a few deep breaths.

Everybody settled in on their cushions. They looked up at Mr. Taylor, waiting eagerly for him to begin. Then their teacher snaked up one of his long arms and turned on the lamp over his big, comfy chair. A picture sprang into view on the lamp shade: Leo saw a seaside town with a harbor full of tall-masted ships. The story was about to start!

"It all started one sunny Sunday morning in September," Mr. Taylor said when he opened his eyes. **"Tom's mother was putting a roast in the oven when he came downstairs."**

The Adventure Begins

Roast *lamb, again?" Tom asked. He was sick* to death of roast lamb every single Sunday. "Of course," his mother answered. And then, without even turning around to look at him, she added, "And you'll need to change into a clean shirt for church."

Tom groaned. "Lucky for me, there's one hanging in my closet, isn't there?"

"Naturally," his mother said. "Wash day was Friday, and I ironed as usual on Saturday. You have a closet full of clean, pressed shirts."

Tom sighed. His mother loved routines and schedules as much as he hated them. Wouldn't it be nice, he thought, if just once they could go for a hike or a row in the harbor on a beautiful Sunday morning? And would it really be so earth-shattering if they had pork chops and applesauce for Sunday dinner, instead of roast lamb and mint jelly? Tom was the only one in the family who seemed to mind. His sisters were just like his mother, down to the particular way they folded the sheets they all helped to wash on Fridays. And Father was so often away on business that he barely seemed to notice.

Still, Tom was a good boy. Someday when he was older, he would be able to do things his own way. But he was only ten, so for now he had to obey his parents.

Later that day, with church and dinner finally over, Tom changed into his favorite old trousers and blue flannel shirt and walked toward the harbor to see which ships were in. He'd loved watching the sailing ships since before he could even walk, and by now he knew many of the ships by sight. His heart beat a little faster as he came to the top of the hill that overlooked the bay. He took a deep breath, smiling as he filled his lungs with the clean, fresh salt air, so different from the stale indoor air he'd been breathing all day. "Hurrah!" he cried out loud as he ran down the cobbled street toward the busy harbor.

The *Fortunata* was at anchor, and so was the *Zephyr*. They were two of Tom's favorite ships, and he'd memorized every inch of their rigging. The *Fortunata* was a three-masted Italian bark, with the third mast a mizzen carrying a spanker and a gaff topsail.

■ ■ ■

"A what?" asked Jennifer.

"He's talking about boats," said Oliver. "Old-fashioned boats, the kind with tall masts and all kinds of different sails. My grandpa builds models of those." He nodded hard, which made his glasses slide down his nose. He pushed them back up.

"They're amazing," Cricket announced. "I've seen them at Oliver's house," she told everybody. "They're really cool."

"But what's all that mizzen-gaff-bark-spanker stuff?" asked Jason. "How are we supposed to know what all that means?"

"How do we usually find out what something means?" asked Mr. Taylor, raising his eyebrows.

"Look it up," Jason answered in a bored, sing-song voice.

"There's a neat book in the library," Oliver said. "It has pictures of all the sailing ships, and it tells you what all the sails are called and what they're for."

"Maybe you can get it at lunchtime and pass it around later on," suggested Mr. Taylor.

"Sure," said Oliver.

"Whatever," said Jennifer. "What about the story?"

"What about it?" asked Mr. Taylor. He gave Jennifer a Look.

Jennifer blushed. "I mean, can you please go on with the story?"

"I'd be happy to," said Mr. Taylor.

■ ■ ■

The Zephyr was a slender, fast frigate built of Malibar teak. On the bow — the front of the ship — was a figurehead picturing the god of the west wind. Another, slightly smaller ship lay beside the *Fortunata*; it was a narrow-beamed clipper that Tom didn't recognize. Judging by its sleek lines, it would be even faster than the magnificent *Zephyr*. As he drew closer, he saw that it was being loaded for a long voyage. Sailors strode up and down the gangway, carrying barrels and boxes and bundles of all shapes and sizes.

"Excuse me," Tom said to one of the men, a stout fellow with a bristly black beard that reminded Tom of a porcupine. "What is this ship, and where is she heading?"

"That's the *Adele*," the man told him. "And we're headed for Barbados as soon as we finish loading her up. We'll sail before noon tomorrow. Going to bring back a load full of molasses and rum."

Barbados! Tom didn't know exactly where that was, but he pictured clear green water and a white sandy beach dotted with palm trees waving in a warm, sweet-smelling tropical breeze. He watched the sailors loading for an hour or so, then realized

he'd better head back home. On Sunday eve-
nings his mother always read aloud to the family,
and he'd catch it if he was late.

That night, Tom could hardly sleep. The image
of palm trees on a sandy beach kept dancing in his
head. Finally, just before dawn, he slipped out of
bed. He pulled on his trousers and shirt and,
holding his shoes, tiptoed downstairs in his stock-
ing feet. He crept into the pantry and loaded an
old flour sack with a tin of crackers, a big hunk
of cheese, a jar of water, and the last half loaf of
raisin-cinnamon bread, the kind his mother baked
every Saturday morning.

Tom scribbled a quick note and left it near the
ironstone sink. He let himself out the back door
into the gray, cold morning. He stood on the steps
for a moment and took a deep breath of the frosty
air. Then, feeling wide awake and more alive than
Tom ever had before, he ran for the harbor.

■ ■ ■

"But —" Molly squeaked. "He can't just run
away from home!" She put her hand over her
mouth. "He's only ten!"

"My cousin ran away from home," Cricket told her. "He was only nine."

"Where did he go?" Leo looked interested.

"Just to his friend's house," Cricket admitted. "He came back in time for dinner. But my aunt was really worried for a few hours."

"Somehow I get the feeling that Tom is not going to be home in time for dinner," said Jason.

"You could be right," said Mr. Taylor, laughing a little. "But I think we're going to have to take a break and get some work done before we find out what happens next."

Everybody groaned.

"Come on," said Mr. Taylor. "You know the deal. Work first, stories later. We'll check in on Tom later today." He reached up and turned off the lamp. "For now, let's get out our spelling list. Who can spell *porcupine*?"

Stowaway!

Leo watched the clock all day, except at lunchtime. Instead of playing kickball at recess, he pored over the book Oliver had brought back from the library until he could picture the ships in the story. He thought the book was cool, even though some of the other kids in class barely looked at it and then made jokes about poop decks.

When he finally saw the little hand on the two and the big hand on the twelve, Leo couldn't stand it anymore. He just had to hear more of his story before school was over for the day. Leo and his science team had finished working on their inventor reports. Leo was writing about Thomas Edison, the guy who invented the lightbulb. But Leo was having trouble concentrating on old Thomas. He couldn't stop wondering what was going to happen next in the story. "Mr. Taylor," he said as they were putting away their folders. "Didn't you say we could hear more of my tale if we did our work?"

"I did, I did," said Mr. Taylor. "And I meant it, too. We have plenty of time before you have to go." After they finished cleaning up the classroom for the day, Mr. Taylor led the way over to the reading corner. He reached up and turned on the light. He took a deep breath. And he dove back into the story.

■ ■ ■

Even though the sun was barely peeking through the pink-and-gold clouds on the horizon, the Adele's crew was already hard at work. From above, the men looked like a swarm of ants bringing food to their nest as they marched up and down the gangplank carrying boxes and parcels and trunks. The sailors were dressed in identical navy blue pants and spanking-clean white shirts. Unnoticed in the early quiet, Tom walked down the street to the pier and stood behind a granite pillar so that he could watch without being seen.

"Look sharp now, there!" called a tall man who was watching the workers from the other side of the dock, his arms folded across his chest. "You'll have to step lively if we want to sail by noon. Did I hire a pack of lazy fools or a crew of sailors? Show me what you can do." His narrow face was pinched with disapproval.

"We're not oxen," grumbled one of the sailors as he passed Tom's pillar. "We can only move so fast when we're carrying a hundred pounds each."

"Captain Blaine wouldn't know about that," sneered another man. "He was born with a silver spoon in his mouth, that one. Never lifted more'n a few ounces in his life, I'll wager."

Tom looked back at the tall, frowning man. So his was the hand at the *Adele*'s helm. Captain Blaine. He did not look like the friendliest fellow. For a moment Tom felt his courage fail him. Back in his room as he lay under a warm, heavy quilt, the idea had seemed so exciting, so adventurous, so completely irresistible. But now he wondered if he was crazy. What would this Captain Blaine do to a boy he caught stowing away on his ship?

For that was Tom's plan. He intended to slip onto the *Adele* and hide until the ship was well out at sea. After a few days, when his food ran out, he would have to reveal himself. But by then, he reasoned, what could they do? Nobody would throw a ten-year-old boy to the sharks. They would put him to work, and he would join the crew, doing whatever tasks they gave him. He would scrub the decks, if that's what they wanted. Or climb the rigging, or polish the brass rails, or peel potatoes for the cook. He'd be a sailor! And before long he'd be seeing the palm trees of Barbados with his own eyes.

Tom only wavered for a moment. In the next second two men walked by, struggling with the weight of the huge wooden crate they carried between them. This was his chance! Tom dashed out from behind the pillar and approached the men. "Need a hand?" he offered. The man at the rear looked surprised at first. Then he nodded. "Why not?" he asked.

Tom stayed on his side of the box, hidden from Captain Blaine's view. Grasping the bottom edge, he grunted as he did his best to help carry the heavy load up the gangplank. He knew his skinny ten-year-old arms weren't making a big difference, but this was his chance to get on board!

"Where's this one going?" asked the sailor in front, a small, wiry man.

"In the hold, with everything else," answered the other.

Tom knew that the hold was storage space below the deck, kind of like the ship's basement.

The wiry man groaned. "It won't be easy to get this down the stairs," he complained. "Boy!" he ordered Tom. "Go down first, and help guide us."

Tom didn't hesitate. He dodged in front of the crate and down the stairs into the hold. Then he shouted out, "To your right! To your left! Now bring it straight on down!"

The men seemed to appreciate the help. When they finally reached the bottom of the stairs, both were panting hard.

"Rest!" called out the man in front, and they let the crate down gently. "I have to think about where to fit this," he said, scratching his head as he looked around the dark, musty, crowded space. Tom looked around, too. He'd never seen so many boxes and barrels in one place. They were stacked higher than his head, all around the cramped hold. He decided there must be enough supplies to feed an army for a year! With all that food, how could anyone object to feeding one small boy? In the dim light of the hold he could just make out the stenciled labels on some of the barrels. **FLOUR. COFFEE. WHISKEY.**

"Anything going in the strong room?" asked the wiry man. Tom knew what a strong room was, too. It was like a big, locked cage where valuable things could be kept safe.

The other shook his head. "Not unless the cook decided to keep some special ingredients in there." He walked over to an oversized cage that was big enough for two men to stand in. Its barred door was locked with a large brass padlock, and a matching key hung on a nail just nearby. The man opened the lock and peered inside. "Empty," he reported, even though Tom and the other man could see that perfectly well for themselves.

Then he locked the door, returned the key to its nail, and turned to gaze at the crate they'd brought below. "Well, gents," he said. "Shall we?"

All three of them grunted as they picked the crate up again and moved it to a spot near the strong room. Just as they put it down, Tom heard the shrill sound of a whistle from above. "All hands on deck!" came a shout.

The wiry man swore. "If this is another drill —" he began.

"No matter," said the other. "We'd better show ourselves before the captain blows up." The two of them headed for the stairs without a second look at Tom.

■ ■ ■

"Wait! They're just going to leave him there?" Leo interrupted. It was cool that the cheese and the brass key had already shown up in the story. But he didn't think it was fair that the men had left Tom without a word.

Mr. Taylor shook his head. "They are. And Tom was just as glad to be forgotten. For, you see, this was his big chance!"

"For what?" Jason asked.

"For hiding," Mr. Taylor said, with a gleam in his eye. And he went on.

■ ■ ■

Ignoring the pounding of feet and the shouted orders from above, Tom looked around wildly, searching for a good hiding place. For a moment, he considered the strong box. But he quickly realized the danger of becoming locked in by mistake. By that time, his eyes were nearly adjusted to the dark, and he could make out all sorts of nooks and crannies that might be right. But how to decide?

Suddenly, Tom felt something brush against his leg. He jumped, gasping. Was he going to have to spend the next few days fighting off rats? Then he heard a familiar rumbling. It was the same sound his cat, Snowflake, made when he petted her soft white fur as she sat on his lap near the fire. He looked down to see a scruffy gray-and-white-striped tomcat rubbing against his leg. "Hello," he whispered as he reached down to scratch the animal's head.

The cat butted up against Tom's hand for a moment, then began to trot toward a dark corner, far back in the hold. Tom followed him. Then the cat disappeared.

Where had he gone? Tom searched among the crates until he heard a tiny chirrup. He squatted down to see the cat. It was sitting there in a small cavelike space created by the corners of three large crates, calmly washing his face with a big gray paw.

"Perfect," said Tom softly, crawling in to curl up next to the cat.

■ ■ ■

The bell rang. School was over. But just for a second, nobody in room 3B moved a muscle. Leo could just picture Tom hiding between the crates in the stuffy, shadowy hold of the ship. "Wow," he breathed. "So he's really going to stow away on the *Adele*?"

Mr. Taylor nodded. "Tom's looking for adventure, and I have a feeling he's going to find it." He stood up and turned off the lamp. "But we'll have to wait until tomorrow to hear what happens next."

Leo Gets Fired

[C]ome on! Why are you so slow today?" Leo's friend Pete had been waiting impatiently on the playground. He was in room 3A, Ms. Porter's class. Now he was trying to rush Leo to soccer practice. "We're going to be late, and you know what Coach Hauser says about that."

Leo knew what Coach would say, all right. He'd heard the lecture over and over again. Not that Coach Hauser had ever been talking to *him*. Leo was always on time, because Leo always ran to practice. His soccer bag would bump against his legs as he dashed from school to the town recreation fields near the river.

But Coach Hauser definitely did have a thing about players being on time. "We can't have an effective practice until everybody's here," he always said. "Plus, you have to get used to being on time. What if you were late on a game day? You'd be letting the team down."

Yeah, yeah, thought Leo as he trudged along. His soccer bag felt heavier than ever. How could a pair of cleats, his shin guards, and a mouth guard weigh so much? For the first time, he wished his mom would pick him up and drive him over to the field like some of the other moms.

"Murray! Peltzman! Just in time!" Coach Hauser said, clapping his hands as Leo and Pete arrived. "I almost gave up on you two."

"Sorry, Coach Hauser," muttered Leo.

"Don't be sorry. Just be early next time!" Coach Hauser said with a grin. He was always smiling, even when he was ticked off. He said he had the best job in the world, because he loved soccer. He had been the star of his high school team, and now he was the goalie for his college team. He had told Leo's team that this was his first time coaching, and he wanted to make sure they loved the game as much as he did.

So far, Leo didn't think he was doing a very good job with that.

Leo tried to smile back. "Right," he said.

"Sure," said Pete. He gave Leo a dirty look, as if he blamed him for making them late.

"Big game tomorrow," said Coach Hauser. "We're playing the Green Giants, and I hear they haven't lost a game yet."

"Dumb name," Pete whispered to Leo.

Leo nodded. He had helped name their team — the Purple Piranhas — but now he thought that name was kind of dumb, too. Fish didn't play soccer. Especially man-eating fish! Leo started to daydream about floating down the Amazon River in a dugout canoe. Piranhas were leaping out of the water on every side, snapping at his hands. But Leo the Brave barely noticed. He just kept paddling onward, toward the treasure he knew was hidden in the jungle.

"Leo? Ahem! Mr. Murray?"

Leo jerked out of his dream. No canoe. No deep, murky river. No piranhas. Just Coach Hauser, snapping his fingers at him.

"Are you with us, Leo?" he asked. "We have lots to work on today. I need everybody's full attention and cooperation."

Leo nodded. "Sorry," he said.

"Don't be sorry," Coach Hauser said with his usual smile. "Just listen up next time."

Leo nodded again.

"Okay, everybody. Let's warm up. Three laps running, one lap dribbling a ball. Let's go!" Coach Hauser clapped his hands. "Leo, wait up," he said when everybody else took off around the field.

Uh-oh. Leo stood stock-still, waiting for Coach Hauser to yell at him.

Instead, he put his hand on Leo's shoulder and looked him in the eye. "Are you all right, Leo?" Coach Hauser asked in a gentle voice. "I don't mean to be hard on you. I'm just trying to make every practice a great practice. And that takes cooperation from everybody."

"Okay," Leo said in a small voice. He should have known. Coach Hauser never exactly yelled.

He was actually a pretty nice guy. He was just way too into rules and drills.

After they'd finished their laps, Coach Hauser had everybody gather near one of the goals. He had set up rows of orange traffic cones in the middle of the field. "We're going to combine some work on passing and dribbling," he said. "Everybody partner up."

Leo and Pete looked at each other and nodded in agreement. They were always partners. They were partners on game days, too, getting the ball to the goal without needing a word of direction. Pete was great at passing the ball to Leo when Leo was in position to shoot for the goal. Coach said Leo needed to work on his passing, too, but Leo didn't think that made much sense. He could pass well enough when he needed to, but meanwhile he and Pete had their routine worked out. Why mess with a good thing?

Coach Hauser explained how the drill would work. One partner would dribble the ball through the cones, weaving in a figure-eight pattern.

The other partner would be standing across the field, waiting for a pass. When the first partner got to the last cone, he would pass the ball to the waiting partner, and that partner would dribble the ball back.

"Fun, huh?" asked Coach Hauser. He smiled hopefully.

"Whatever," Leo said under his breath.

Coach Hauser gave him a sharp look.

Leo didn't really even care. He just wanted to *play*! Why did they have to do all these stupid drills? Most of the guys had been practicing dribbling and passing since they were about four years old.

Coach Hauser shrugged. "I know it's not the most exciting drill, but these basics are incredibly important. We'll use them in every game." He clapped his hands. "So let's get started!"

Leo trudged toward the cones, feeling so bored he could hardly stand it.

Practice seemed to last forever that afternoon. They did more dribbling and passing drills, some shooting drills, some sprints. *At least we have a game tomorrow,* Leo thought as he packed up his stuff. Finally, some playing!

But Coach Hauser had other ideas. "Leo," he said, coming over to kneel next to Leo's soccer bag. "I have a feeling you'd rather not be here. Is that right?"

Leo shrugged.

"I think you might be a little burned out on soccer," said Coach Hauser. "You might need to take a step back and think over whether you really want to stay on the team."

Leo stared at him. "What?"

"I need players with enthusiasm and energy," said Coach Hauser. "I'm not feeling that from you. Not at all. I suggest that you take tomorrow off. Come to the game if you want, but I'm not going to put you in. I want you to take some time to think over your commitment to the team."

Leo could not believe his ears. It was true that he had been thinking about quitting, but now it was like Coach Hauser was firing him!

He was speechless.

Coach Hauser looked at him. "I'm not doing this to punish you, Leo. Do you understand?"

Leo barely managed to nod.

"Good," said Coach Hauser. "And Leo? I really hope you'll decide to stay on the team. You're the best shooter in the league. We really need good players like you."

Tom Has Second Thoughts

At sharing time the next day, Leo was still thinking about what Coach Hauser had said. He couldn't believe it! Just because he was a little distracted at practice, he was getting cut from the team.

Okay, if he was honest with himself, he knew that wasn't exactly fair. But still! Was he supposed to *love* those dumb drills?

He didn't have his soccer bag with him. He wasn't sure if he was even going to go to the game that afternoon. He wasn't sure he could stand watching if he couldn't play. He frowned at the floor, imagining himself on the sidelines.

"Leo?" Mr. Taylor asked. "Any decision about soccer?"

"Huh?" asked Leo. He'd been so lost in his thoughts that he hadn't even noticed that sharing time had been under way for a few minutes. "Um, no."

"Still thinking about it, then?" asked Mr. Taylor.

Leo just nodded. He saw his friend Cricket looking at him curiously, but he didn't look back. He didn't feel like explaining what had happened.

"Well," said Mr. Taylor, leaning back in his chair. "If nobody has any other pressing news to report, perhaps we could get back to Tom's story."

Leo brightened. Anything to take his mind off soccer! "Yeah!" he yelled, along with everybody else.

Mr. Taylor put his fingertips together and smiled. "Good," he said. "I hated to leave him hiding in the hold like that. So cramped." He reached up to turn on the lamp. Then he began.

■ ■ ■

Tom must have fallen asleep, for the next thing he knew, he woke with a start, banging his head hard on the sharp corner of a crate. "Ouch!" he said softly, rubbing his forehead.

The gray cat chirruped and rubbed his head against Tom's knee.

"You're still here?" Tom gathered the cat up in his arms. He didn't squirm. Far from it. The big tomcat curled up happily, purring so loudly Tom was almost afraid someone would hear it and find him.

But there was nobody nearby. Footsteps pounded on the deck overhead, but the hold was quiet and still. The *Adele* must be fully loaded and almost ready to set sail.

The cat reached up a big paw to touch Tom's face, and Tom grabbed it gently. "Six toes!" he said, looking at the paw closely in the dim light.

■ ■ ■

"I knew it!" said Leo. "I had a feeling that cat was going to have six toes, since that's what I asked for."

"Hmm," said Mr. Taylor. "And here I thought the cat had six toes because that's what he was born with." He grinned and went on with the story.

■ ■ ■

Just then, there was a creaking as the ship, whose movement had been gentle up until then, tilted hard to starboard. Tom froze. The cat jumped out of his arms. "We're under sail!" he said under his breath. His heart thumped in his chest. For a split second he pictured his mother reaching for the note on the sink when she came down to start cooking breakfast. He shook his head and thought of white sand and green water, instead.

Barbados! It would be the first stop on a lifetime of adventure. For now that Tom was aboard a moving ship, he knew that a life at sea was just what he wanted. Even down there in the dark, dank hold, he could feel the thrill of being aboard a ship, bound for adventure.

The ship leaned to one side again, sending Tom sprawling against a crate. The cat let out a short yowl in protest when Tom landed on him. "Sorry," Tom whispered.

His stomach flipped over, and he felt hot all over, then cold. It reminded him of the way he'd felt last summer after he had eaten some bad clams.

For a moment he wondered if he was going to be sick. What could be worse? A seasick stowaway would be the laughingstock of the ship. Not to mention that Tom's life as a sailor would be cut short. How could he spend his life aboard ships if he felt this way every time he felt the motion of the waves? Maybe he just wasn't cut out to be a sailor.

Tom sat very still for a few minutes, and soon the feeling passed. In fact, he began to feel hungry again. A good sign! He nibbled on the raisin bread he had brought, and had a sip of water.

Above him, Tom heard the sound of the ship's bell clanging the hour. Then a whistle blew, and soon footsteps pounded on the deck over Tom's head as the crew responded to an order Tom could not hear.

The echo of shouted orders drifted down into the hold. Tom could not hear the words, but the tone was angry and demanding. He pictured Blaine's narrow, mean face. What would that face look like when it gazed upon a young stowaway?

Stomping footsteps and the bang of musket butts shook the deck as the men drilled in response to the captain's orders. Tom knew what they were doing: They were practicing how to fight back if pirates boarded the ship. Though the days of Blackbeard were long over, there were still pirates on the high seas. A crew must be armed and trained if they were to defend their ship.

The drills went on and on. Tom could feel the pounding of marching feet throughout the *Adele*'s timbers. Or was that his own heart pounding?

Suddenly, he could not help wondering if he had made an enormous mistake.

What Tom Overheard

Mr. Taylor paused to pour some water into his mug and take a drink.

Leo loved Tom's story so far, but as soon as Mr. Taylor stopped, Leo's mind immediately drifted to soccer. Right then Leo thought he knew exactly how Tom felt. He was wondering the same thing himself. Was it an enormous mistake to think about quitting soccer? Leo still couldn't decide whether he should go to the game that afternoon, knowing that Coach Hauser was not going to put him in to play.

On the one hand, he knew it would be really hard to watch everybody else play when he couldn't.

On the other, what else was he going to do? Sit at home and feel even *more* left out?

Mr. Taylor put down his mug and went back to

the story. Leo gave his head a little shake. Forget soccer! He wanted to hear more about Tom.

■ ■ ■

Tom was cold. The drills had been over for a long time. Tom could hear the ship's bells, the ones that told the time. The sound was too faint to make out. Was it midnight? Afternoon? It was always dark, down in the hold. How long had he been aboard the *Adele*? Tom had been drifting in and out of a restless sleep, eating small pieces of cracker and tiny lumps of cheese only when he was too hungry to wait another minute.

The cat had come and gone several times. In between, Tom had heard rustlings and squeaks and sudden thumps, and he knew that the cat was busy hunting. Tom shivered when he thought of the brown, scaly-tailed creatures that scurried all over the hold. He hoped the cat would keep any rats far away from him.

Tom was stiff and sore from sitting in his hiding place. Slowly, he wriggled his way out in order to stretch a bit, but before he'd walked three steps he heard the hatch open. Moments later, two sailors came down into the hold, talking about how they'd been sent by the cook to find a barrel of oats.

Tom dove back into his cave between the crates. His heart was beating wildly.

"What's that?" one of the men asked.

"Rats, probably," answered the other. "Or old Willy. He prowls this hold day and night, he does."

Willy? For a moment, Tom couldn't imagine who they were talking about. Then he realized it must be the gray cat. Willy. Tom smiled in the dark. Now he knew his friend's name.

"Lucky animal," the first man said. "Living down here far from Blaine's constant nagging and yelling. I tell you, I won't put up with that bully forever."

"No need to think about forever," the other said soothingly. "This voyage won't last more than three months."

"Blaine won't last more than three days if he keeps treating us so badly," muttered the first man. "And I know at least five sailors who agree with me."

There was a brief silence.

"Are you speaking of mutiny?" Suddenly, Tom recognized that voice. It was the big man with the porcupine beard, the one he'd talked to on the dock.

"You said the word first," was the answer.

"Aye, I said the word," said the stout man. "But I'll not do the deed. Mutiny is serious business. The punishment for being caught is . . . well, it's not worth the risk, to my way of thinking."

Tom could hardly believe his ears. Mutiny! Was this sailor serious about taking over the ship? Would he kill Captain Blaine? What would become of a stowaway who found himself among mutineers?

Tom's mind raced as he listened to the men talk. They found the oats and headed back up, closing the hatch behind them. Tom was alone again in the dark, crowded hold. Even Willy was no comfort now.

Tom Gets Hungry

When Mr. Taylor paused, Molly raised her hand. Leo thought it was funny that she just couldn't break that habit, even though Mr. Taylor didn't require it. "What's *mutiny*?" she asked. "I never heard that word before."

"I know!" said Jason. "I saw a movie about it once."

"Want to explain?" asked Mr. Taylor.

Jason told how sometimes, in the old days, sailors on a ship would get tired of following their captain's orders. "Like, if he was too mean, or if he didn't know what he was doing," he said. The sailors would decide that they were better off sailing the ship themselves. Sometimes all of the sailors were in on the plot, sometimes only a few. "Usually there was a big fight," Jason said, his eyes gleaming. "Guys would get thrown over-board to the sharks and stuff."

Leo wondered if he should lead a mutiny against Coach Hauser. Maybe if everybody on the soccer team decided they were tired of his dumb drills, they could take over the team and run things themselves. He wished he had thought of that. Instead, he was on his own, the only one who wasn't going to be allowed to play that day. He felt as if *he* had been thrown to the sharks. Leo frowned.

Mr. Taylor thanked Jason, then reached up to turn off the lamp. "Later!" he promised when everybody begged him to go on with the story.

The day passed quickly — too quickly for Leo, who for once was not looking forward to school being over. That just meant it was time for his soccer game, and he still had not decided what to do. Leo was happy toward the end of the day when Mr. Taylor announced that it was time to catch up with Tom. Cool! Two story times in one day. Mr. Taylor seemed to be enjoying telling the story as much as they were enjoying hearing it.

Leo ran over with the others to grab a pillow and get ready to listen.

"Now, where was I?" Mr. Taylor asked. Leo had a feeling the teacher was only pretending not to know, but he joined everybody else in yelling out what he remembered.

"The ship started sailing!" Jason shouted, "And —"

"Tom got sick!" Cricket finished.

"The cat was there," said Leo. "His name is Willy."

"Then the sailors started talking about munity!" said Jennifer.

Everybody cracked up. *Mutiny!* Jason corrected his sister.

"And Tom was scared," Molly put in.

Mr. Taylor nodded. "Right," he said. "Tom was definitely pretty scared." He went back to the story.

■ ■ ■

Tom did not sleep much after overhearing the men talk about mutiny. How could he? The whole idea was terrifying. There was sure to be fighting and bloodshed. Tom lay curled up in his hiding place. He was miserable. He was afraid. And he was wide awake.

Willy bumped his head against Tom's knee and purred as loudly as a cat can purr. Tom scratched his friend's ears, but his mind was on other matters.

Food, for instance. Tom was very, very hungry.

■ ■ ■

"But he's down in the storeroom!" Cricket said. "There's food all around him."

"First of all," Mr. Taylor answered, "that food didn't belong to him. Taking it would be stealing, and Tom knew that. But that wasn't the only thing that stopped him."

■ ■ ■

It was almost funny. He was surrounded by hundreds of pounds of food, and Tom was hungrier than he'd ever been in his life. What good was a fifty-pound bag of flour or a barrel of dried beans? He couldn't eat those things. They weren't cooked! No, Tom only had the food he had carried aboard, and it was running out fast.

He'd nibbled at the crackers until all that was left was a small pile of stale crumbs. The cheese was long gone. Tom had worried that it would mold quickly and be wasted, so he had allowed himself a tiny chunk every time he heard the ship's bell clang. He'd only sipped at his water, but there was barely an inch left in the jar. Tom's throat was parched.

The only thing left to eat was the cinnamon bread, and Tom was saving that. It was already getting hard and stale, but he knew that the dark, plump raisins would stay soft and delicious for at least another day. His dry mouth watered a little as he thought of their chewy sweetness, and he could almost smell the warm, spicy scent of cinnamon that wafted through the house whenever his mother baked this bread.

He checked again to see how much he had. Nearly half a loaf. He'd only let himself tear off one small piece so far. How long would half a loaf last? Two days? Three? Could it keep him alive for a whole week? Tom didn't think so. He didn't know how long he had been in the hold, but he was already weak with hunger. Half a loaf of bread, no matter how full of raisins, was not enough to keep a boy alive for very long.

The ship was well out of the harbor and moving along, probably sailing a southerly course down the coast. Tom guessed they could be as far south as Maryland already. He had planned to come out of hiding after a day or two. But with mutiny hanging in the air, this was not the time for Tom to show himself.

He held his breath and listened. What was going on above him? Were the men gathering secretly in the foredeck, cleaning their guns and plotting revenge on Captain Blaine? If the mutiny was going to happen, Tom thought, it had better happen soon — before he starved.

Mutiny!

Then it began.

Tom heard it all from the hold: the two loud shots, the sudden shouting, the running up and down the deck.

Mutiny.

Tom had read stories about mutiny at sea. None of them ever ended well. It was serious business to take over a ship. Some mutineers were killed during the attempted rebellion. Other mutineers succeeded, but were arrested at the next port and, after a short trial, hung. A few escaped for years and years, sailing to ever more distant lands to escape the law. Of those, most were eventually chased down and hung. None of them ever reached a happy old age.

The captains didn't fare much better. Often, mutineers just murdered the captain in cold blood.

Other commanders were set adrift in a small boat with few provisions or left ashore on a desert island with only enough water for a day.

Tom felt as if he could hardly breathe. He did not dare to move from his hiding place; in fact, he hardly dared to move a muscle until he knew what had happened.

It wasn't long before he realized one thing: The captain was still alive. Only minutes after the commotion above, the hatch flew open and several men struggled down the ladder, carrying something heavy. The heavy thing was kicking and shouting, and even in the dim light it wasn't hard for Tom to tell that it was tall Captain Blaine. His arms were tied behind his back. His shouts were muffled because of the rag stuffed in his mouth, but one thing was clear: He was angry.

The men carried Blaine over to the steel-banded strong room, shoved him inside, slammed the door, and turned the big brass key in the lock.

"He looks like a gorilla in the zoo!" one of the men said, laughing as he stared through the barred door.

"He won't be making monkeys of *us* any longer," said another.

The third man reached an arm inside and pulled the rag out of the captain's mouth. "Nobody down here to hear his ranting," he said.

They watched the captain shout and wrestle with his ropes for a few minutes, then they put the key back on its hook on the side of the strong room and headed back up the ladder. On their way, they grabbed a cask of whiskey. "We'll anchor at Clayson's Cove tonight and have ourselves a high old time," said one of the men as they carried the cask up the ladder.

Tom was still frozen in place. So much had happened so quickly! He looked at the man in the strong room. Captain Blaine was red-faced and breathing hard. No matter how harsh he'd been, it didn't seem right for him to be held in a pen like an animal.

It was Tom's leg that finally gave him away, his right one. It had fallen so fast asleep that he could barely move it, and when he did, he couldn't help letting out a gasp as the pins and needles came on full force. Tom's movement and his gasp woke Willy from a nap. The cat rose and stretched, then sauntered over to the strong room and began to rub himself on the bars of the door. He leaned hard against them as he stalked back and forth. His purr filled the hold with sound.

"Willy!" Tom saw the captain struggle to a seated position and reach a hand through the bars. "Wills, my boy! Good to see you!"

Was Willy the captain's cat? Tom couldn't help feeling better about the man if he cared so much for Willy. Blaine's voice was friendly and soft when he talked to the big cat.

"Ouch!" Tom squeaked without thinking as he moved his other leg; that one was asleep, too.

"Who's there?" Captain Blaine looked around, peering through the bars of his prison. His voice was harsh again.

Truly, Tom realized, he had nothing to lose. Facing this man was no longer his greatest fear. Captain Blaine was not the one making the decisions aboard the *Adele*. Not anymore.

"It's me," Tom said, crawling out of his hiding place on stiff, painful legs. "Tom. I'm a —"

"Stowaway," Captain Blaine finished, staring at him. "A young one, too. Even younger than I was on my first voyage." He didn't seem all that surprised to see a boy pop out from behind the crates.

"You were a stowaway?" Tom gaped at the man.

The captain nodded. "Once upon a time, yes, I was." He smiled, and for the first time Tom thought there might be more to this man than he'd seen and heard before. "I stowed away when I was just twelve years old. I hid aboard the *Johanna*, a frigate sailing for Cape Horn."

"What happened when you were found?" Tom asked.

"Oh, the captain wasn't any too happy at first," Blaine said. "But I soon proved my worth. There wasn't a sailor on that ship who could climb a mast as fast as I could, and in any kind of weather."

Captain Blaine looked off into the distance, as if

he were seeing the open sea instead of the dim, crate-packed hold. "I haven't spent more than a few nights at a time on dry land since then," he said. "Lived my life on ships, I have. And I have loved every minute of it."

His eyes had lit up for a moment, but now they darkened again. "It looks as if I'll spend both the beginning and the end of my career hidden in the hold," he muttered.

"Can't you get the ship back?" Tom asked. "Was every man on the crew against you?"

"I don't know," Blaine answered wryly. "I was too busy fighting them off to count." He wriggled his arms inside the ropes, which were beginning to loosen. "It seems the crew prefers revelry to sailing. But I'll tell you one thing: If we anchor at Clayson's Cove tonight, I'll wager the new command will get more of a party than they bargain for."

"What do you mean?" Tom asked.

Captain Blaine's face was stony as he gave a one-word answer. "Pirates."

Piranhas vs. Giants

Everybody looked at Leo when Mr. Taylor said the word *pirates*. They all remembered back in second grade when Leo had been totally, completely, pirate-crazy. It had all started when his mom took him to the eye doctor. Dr. Jenkins had said that Leo had a lazy eye and that he should wear a patch over his good eye to make his lazy eye work harder.

Leo did not like that plan.

So his mom got the idea of getting him a pirate sword and hat and a pirate chest for his treasure (Legos, mostly). That way, the patch was just all part of a whole pirate theme.

Leo liked that plan a little better.

In fact, he liked it so much that he ended up wearing his pirate gear all the time. He got a stuffed parrot named Matey that he carried around, too.

And he talked pirate talk. "Aye, me hearty," he would answer when his mom asked if he wanted more French toast for breakfast. "Ahoy!" he would shout when he saw his dad coming up the walk.

His parents got kind of tired of it.

So did his teachers.

And his friends.

And finally, so did Leo.

The pirate thing had been fun, but it was, as his mom had often hoped, just a phase. Now Leo was much more interested in other things, like soccer and bugs. But he still had a soft spot for pirates. Just hearing the word in the middle of this story gave him goose bumps. He should have known there would be pirates — after all, he had asked for a pirate ship, hadn't he? But somehow it was still a surprise to hear that they were about to appear.

"Pirates," he repeated softly after Mr. Taylor said it.

"Right, pirates," answered Mr. Taylor. "But" — he checked the clock on the wall — "not until tomorrow. For now we'll have to leave Tom and

Captain Blaine in the hold. That'll give them time to get to know each other."

Leo looked up at the clock. School was over. It was time for the soccer game.

Leo stood for a long time staring into his cubby, trying to decide whether to go to the field or not. Finally, he slammed the door, leaving his soccer bag inside, and headed out the side door. Pete had already left, so Leo headed to the field by himself. And for once, he didn't run. He walked. Slowly. Twice he almost turned around, but finally, he arrived at the field.

"I didn't think you were coming!" said Pete when he saw Leo. "I would have waited for you." Pete knew all about what had happened at practice the day before.

Leo waved his hand. "No problem. I didn't think I was coming, either."

"Glad you did," said Coach Hauser, coming up behind them. "Want to warm up with the team?"

Leo glanced toward the field and saw some of his teammates, dressed in their Purple Piranhas T-shirts, running laps. The rest of them had finished running and were stretching on the sidelines.

The Green Giants were stretching at the other end of the field. Usually, when Leo saw the other team warming up, he got a sort of jumpiness in his stomach. "Butterflies," his mom called it. It was a kind of nervous feeling, but a good one, too.

Today there were no butterflies. Leo felt more as if he had a toad in his stomach. He watched as Pete ran over to join in the stretching.

"Leo?" Coach Hauser was still waiting for an answer.

"No, I guess not," said Leo.

"Okay," Coach Hauser said, shrugging. He bent over and started pulling soccer balls out of a bag. One of the balls rolled toward the field, and Leo automatically put out his foot to stop it. He rolled it back and forth under his foot for a moment. It felt so familiar! Leo had been kicking soccer balls around since he was just a tiny little kid.

He started dribbling it up and down the sidelines, practicing direction changes now and then.

He hated to admit it, but Coach was right in some ways about his passing game being a little weak. He was a good dribbler, but he wished he could pass as well as Pete. He got so involved in what he was doing that the starting whistle came as a surprise. When he looked out at the field, he saw both teams set to play. Pete was in Leo's usual position, playing forward.

Leo felt the toad in his stomach take a hop or two. He almost didn't want to watch. But he couldn't help himself. He stood near Coach Hauser on the sidelines, following every movement of the players and the ball.

"Nice pass," he muttered when Jacob kicked a long one to Pete.

"Good save!" he shouted when their goalie, Paulie, stopped a high-flying ball from speeding into the net.

"Come on," he urged as Pete dribbled the ball up the field, working his way toward the goal.

The team was playing fairly well, but somehow they weren't making progress. By the end of the first half, the Green Giants were ahead, 2–0.

Pete came over to Leo during halftime. "Miss you out there," he said, panting a little. He had been running hard. "You better make up your mind and come back to play unless you want to see us lose *all* our games. We need a good shooter like you. Jacob's getting better, but he's no Leo."

After the half, the pace of the game picked up even more. The Green Giants were working hard on defense, and Leo's teammates couldn't get the ball anywhere near the goal. Instead, their defenders were working overtime trying to keep the Green Giants from scoring. Soon the score was 3–0.

"What's the problem?" Leo heard Coach Hauser mutter. "The drills definitely helped their passing skills, and their footwork is excellent."

"Right," said Leo, who was standing right next to him. "But . . ."

"But what?" asked Coach Hauser. "Do you have an idea about how to get them to score?"

"Well," said Leo, "Maybe if you put Jacob on defense and moved Dylan to forward. He and Pete used to play together a lot last year. They can usually move the ball upfield until one or the other of them can get a shot."

"Just like you and Pete," Coach Hauser said, nodding. "Thanks for the tip. Anything else?"

Leo liked being asked. "Jake loves playing guard," he said. "If you put him near our goal, they won't get nearly as many shots."

"Huh!" Coach Hauser said. And as soon as he could, he called for a time-out. After the coach had a quick chat with the team, the game started again. Coach Hauser had made all the changes Leo suggested. And this time he seemed to pay a little more attention to the *players* than to their skills. "Go, Jake!" he yelled, along with Leo. "Take it, Pete!"

The guys noticed, too. With the coach's encouragement, they ran faster and kicked the ball farther.

The Piranhas came back strong after the time-out. They still lost the game, but the final score was 3–2. Not bad for a game against the best team in the league.

Once again, Coach Hauser asked Leo to stay behind after all the cheering, high-fiving, and packing up was over.

"I guess drills aren't everything," the coach admitted, looking a little sheepish. "You really helped bring the team to life. Tell you what, Leo," he said. "If you decide you'd rather not play anymore, I could sure use an assistant coach. You know a lot about your teammates and about the game. You could be a real help to me."

Leo was flattered. He realized once again that Coach Hauser was not a bad guy. He was just new at the job, and he was trying to figure it out. But Leo didn't really want to be an assistant coach. He wanted to be out there on the field taking passes from Pete and kicking the ball into the goal. Score!

"Um," said Leo. "Thanks. I guess I'm still thinking about it." For a second he wondered if he could tell Coach Hauser why he had been acting so distracted at practice. "You know those drills?" he added. "They do help. Really. But — they're boring!" He couldn't believe he was saying it out loud. But who else was going to say it? "Everybody hates them," he added, so the coach would know it wasn't just him.

It wasn't exactly a mutiny. But Coach needed to hear it. Otherwise Leo wouldn't be the only Piranha thinking about quitting. Leo wondered if Coach Hauser was going to get mad at him for speaking up.

But Coach looked at him and nodded. "I see," he said. Then he started scooping soccer balls into a duffel bag. "Well, I guess you better decide soon," said Coach Hauser. "Whether you're playing or helping me coach, we have three more games coming up. See you at practice on Friday?"

Leo nodded. He understood. By Friday, he would have to decide what he was going to do. If he didn't want to coach, he either had to give up playing soccer — or play by Coach Hauser's rules.

What's that Sound?

Leo didn't sleep well that night. He tossed and turned, trying to figure out what to do about soccer. Should he quit the team? Or should he stay on it and be bored? Or should he become the assistant coach? He was still a little groggy when he got to school, but he woke up fast after sharing time when Mr. Taylor turned on the lamp in the reading corner and began the story again. Tom's adventure was getting more exciting all the time.

■ ■ ■

Tom and Captain Blaine talked quietly down in the hold, one inside the cage and one out. Tom could see the big brass key hanging from its ring on the outside of the strong room, but somehow he didn't quite trust Blaine, not enough to set him free. For now, it felt safer to stay hidden and wait to see what happened next.

What happened next was commotion. First, Tom heard the anchor go overboard, a running of chains ending in a big splash. Were they in Clayson's Cove? Tom had no way of knowing. But the sounds of celebration that followed were unmistakable. Judging by the shouts and laughter and the thundering sound of feet jigging to a hornpipe, the men had opened that cask of whiskey and were making their way through it quickly.

Captain Blaine did not seem to care. Not about the party above their heads, nor about the possibility of getting his ship back. He didn't mention pirates again. He just sighed and talked about his wife. "Ah, my sweet Agnes," he'd say. "Will I ever see her and my two darling daughters again? Will the girls remember their papa?"

Finally, he drifted off into sleep, leaving Tom to listen alone to the party above. There was something frightening about the shouts of the men, even though they sounded like shouts of happiness. Tom was not happy to be aboard a ship that was in the hands of these foolish, easily angered scoundrels. Did they even know how to sail the

Adele properly? Captain Blaine might not have been the kindest man or the best leader, but at least he was an experienced sailor.

Tom began to drift off himself, sitting there outside the strong room with Willy in his lap. But something woke him up. A bump. The ship shuddered as it took a blow to the side. Suddenly, there was a different tone to the shouts from above. The laughter had stopped. Now the voices were panicked. Other voices joined in, and there was the sound of running feet as the crew raced off in every direction.

Tom reached through the bars and shook Captain Blaine awake. "Listen. What's happening? What are those sounds?" There was a scrabbling on the side of the boat, and a thumping on the deck over their heads.

■ ■ ■

"I know!" Leo yelled.

"So did Blaine," Mr. Taylor told him.

■ ■ ■

Blaine rubbed his eyes. "We're being boarded," he answered.

Pirates!

Tom stared at him.

"Pirates," Captain Blaine said. "No seasoned captain would ever think of anchoring at Clayson's Cove." He shook his head. "There've been pirates in the Carolinas for as long as anyone can remember. The families on the mainland support themselves by piracy and by scavenging shipwrecks."

"But," Tom began, "what will they do?" Tom had seen pictures of pirates and read about them in books. The stories were entertaining. But the idea of coming face-to-bearded-face with a real pirate — a pirate armed with a musket, or swinging a sharp cutlass — that was just plain scary.

"Steal everything they can lay their hands on," Captain Blaine answered with a bitter smile. "And they'll probably kill us all and scuttle the ship to hide their tracks."

Suddenly, Tom thought he might throw up. He knew what scuttling a ship meant. Sinking it! Was the *Adele* going to end up on the ocean floor? For a moment he was grateful that there was nothing in his stomach. "But the men will fight," he began.

The Captain let out a short bark of a laugh. "The men," he said, "if you can call them that, are probably cowering in whatever dark corners they can find. Their weapons are in a big pile in the bow, where they threw them down after the mutiny. They're in no condition to fight off a boatload of desperate blackguards." He shook his head. "No, they won't put up much of a fight. And before you know it, the pirates will find their way down here and kill us both."

Tom gulped. This was not what he had pictured when he boarded the *Adele*. He had been so full of excitement and so ready for adventure. What would it do to his poor mother if she never saw or heard from him again? He pictured his note again, the few scrawled sentences that would stand forever as his last words to her.

"Maybe they won't find us," he said hopefully.

"Not much room to hide in here," Captain Blaine said, looking around his cell. "They'll surely find me, anyway."

"I'll let you out."

Blaine raised an eyebrow.

"I know where the key is," Tom confessed. "I'm sorry. I should have let you out before."

Captain Blaine just shrugged, as if nothing really mattered anymore. Tom went around to the side of the strong room, took the big brass key off its hook, and let the door swing open.

"There's a drawknife in my pocket," Blaine said to Tom, nodding downward. "It'll make short work of these ropes."

Tom found the knife and sawed away. When the captain was freed, Blaine stood for a moment, rubbing his wrists.

Meanwhile, the noises continued from above.

Shouts and thumping and, suddenly, three shots, one right after the other. *Bang! Bang! Bang!*

"They're overpowering the crew quickly," said Blaine. "They'll be coming down the hatch any minute. We have to disappear! Show me where you were hiding when we first set sail."

Tom would not have guessed that there was room, but somehow he and Blaine and Willy managed to squeeze themselves into the dark hidden corner between the crates. And they did it just in time. Seconds later, the hatch flew open, and several men came down the ladder.

The men were bearded and dressed in colorful rags. They had cutlasses slung at their hips and pistols shoved into their waistbands.

They smelled rank, like wild animals.

They were pirates.

And they were carrying something heavy.

■ ■ ■

Jennifer gasped. "They killed somebody! It's a body!"

"Man, things were tough back then," said Jason.

Cricket shuddered. "Now Tom is going to have to be down in the hold with a dead body," she said.

Leo wanted them all to shut up so Mr. Taylor could get on with the story. He glanced at Mr. Taylor, who was waiting patiently. "Can you guys all just, um, quiet down?" Leo asked. (Mr. Taylor didn't allow the words *shut up* in room 3B.) "Maybe he's *not* dead. But we'll never find out if you don't let Mr. Taylor finish telling what happened."

For a second everybody just looked at Leo. Then they seemed to realize that he was right, and they all fell silent.

Mr. Taylor went on with the story.

The Plot

Wait!" *The heavy thing turned out to be a* man, a *live* man who began to struggle and shout just as Captain Blaine had during his own trip down into the hold. Tom recognized the voice. It was the man he'd heard plotting mutiny as he looked for the flour. The pirates held him tightly.

"That's my first mate," Captain Blaine said into Tom's ear. "Mister Ridley. He led the mutiny."

"You don't understand!" Ridley was shouting as he twisted and kicked, trying to squirm out of his captors' grip. "Ask your leader. Ask O'Hara! We had an agreement."

Tom turned to look at Captain Blaine. What was this? Had the first mate made a deal with the pirates? How could he betray the rest of the crew that way?

The captain's eyes were hard with anger.

Tom didn't even need him to explain. In a flash, he understood the whole thing. The mutiny was nothing but a big fake! Mister Ridley had talked the men into it just so he could sail the ship into Clayson's Cove. Then he encouraged them to lay down their weapons so they wouldn't be able to fight when O'Hara and his band of pirates came on board. What a dirty trick!

"I agreed to sail the ship into your cove," Ridley went on desperately as the men hurried him toward the strong room.

Tom and Captain Blaine nodded at each other. Their eyes met in the dim light of the hold. It was true!

"It was a fair deal!" Ridley went on. "If I delivered the ship, O'Hara was supposed to split his booty with me. I demand my share!"

The three men laughed uproariously. "Oh, you'll get your share, all right," one of them growled. "Your share of misery."

Another one let out a nasty cackle as he shook his head at Ridley. "Didn't your mother ever tell you not to trust a pirate?"

All three howled with laughter again as they thrust Ridley into the strong room, slammed the door shut, locked it, and stomped back up the ladder.

Mister Ridley was left to stare around at the strong room in disbelief. Not only had he been betrayed, manhandled, and insulted, but now he saw that he was in the locked cell — alone! Tom watched from his hiding place. He could see the exact moment when Ridley figured it out: Somehow, Blaine had escaped.

After a moment or two, Blaine stood up and walked out of his hiding place. "That's two big mistakes you've made," Blaine said to his first mate as he strolled over to the strong room. "One, you plotted with a pirate. And the other, you tried to take over a ship when you have no idea what being a captain truly means."

Ridley gaped at Blaine through the bars. "How did you —"

"Never mind," Blaine barked. "The question is, what will we do to save our skins? Not that yours is worth saving. But a captain hates to see any of his crew lost."

■ ■ ■

Mr. Taylor stopped and looked around at his audience. Everybody was staring up at him, mouths open.

"But how could Mister Ridley *do* that?" Cricket squeaked.

"Didn't he have any loyalty to the rest of the crew?" asked Jason. "That's really lame."

"Now he probably expects Captain Blaine to save him," said Jennifer. "That's not fair."

"No, it isn't," said Mr. Taylor.

Leo had not said a word. He stared down at his hands, thinking. He had a feeling Mr. Taylor was looking at him, but he kept his head down.

He felt awful. How could he have been thinking of quitting soccer? That was almost as bad as what Mister Ridley had done. The Purple Piranhas were a team — *his* team. Most of them had been playing soccer together for years, even before they were all Piranhas. Was he really going to ditch them just because he didn't like the way Coach Hauser ran practices? There had to be a better answer. Quitting — betraying his teammates like Mister Ridley had betrayed his crew — was not the right thing to do.

Nobody could believe it when Mr. Taylor said it was time to get some work done. How could they wait to find out what was going to happen to Tom? How could they leave him down there in that hold, with pirates swarming all over the ship? It was Friday, too. If Mr. Taylor didn't finish the story, they were going to have to spend the whole weekend in suspense.

Mr. Taylor shrugged. "The story will wait," he said. "But Ms. Buckley won't. You have music class this morning, and we have a spelling test and some math homework to go over. I promise, though, if you work hard, we'll finish the story today. How does that sound?"

Mr. Taylor didn't even wait for an answer. He just reached up and turned off the lamp.

Tom Makes a Plan

Mr. Taylor's class went to music. They took their spelling test. They went over their math homework. The whole time, they were waiting and wondering. What would happen next to Tom? Fortunately, Mr. Taylor always kept his promises. Later that afternoon, he switched the lamp back on and dove right into the story.

■ ■ ■

Captain Blaine frowned as he paced up and down in the only open space, a tiny area near the strong room. "You know, now that I think about it, not one man of this crew deserves to be saved. Did any of them step forward when I needed their help? Not one. Not one."

He paced and muttered, sounding angrier and angrier.

Finally, Tom couldn't hold his tongue any longer. "No!" he cried as he crawled out from between the crates. "They don't deserve it. But if we don't at least *try* to take back the ship, we'll all be lost."

Mister Ridley looked surprised when Tom jumped out of the hiding place, but only for a moment. After all he'd been through, nothing was likely to surprise him much. "What do we have here? A stowaway?" he asked.

Blaine nodded curtly.

"Hmmm," said Mister Ridley. "Well, the boy is right," he said. "We must try."

"We?" Blaine asked. "I don't need help from the likes of you. A mutineer and a turncoat nobody can trust! You'll stay in the brig here and take your chances when I tell the men how you betrayed them."

Ridley howled, pleading forgiveness, but Blaine ignored him. He turned to Tom. "Supposing you are right that we must try, how do you propose we proceed? We've neither weapons nor an armed crew. There is nothing but confusion and chaos on the upper decks, and we have no idea how many of those pirates have boarded."

"We'll go up together," Tom suggested. "I'll head straight to the bow and gather as many weapons as I can. You'll muster the men."

Blaine snorted. "Muster the men? They're scattered all over the ship, running for their lives. How can I muster the men?"

"With the very routine they rebelled against," Tom said. "I heard you shouting orders all the time. The men may not have wanted to obey, but they did. You trained them well. We can use that training now."

Blaine gave him a considered look. "You may be a captain yet," he said. "I'm not sure I had your cleverness when I was a stowaway."

The captain drew a long breath and seemed to grow taller. He looked more like the man Tom remembered seeing when he first boarded the *Adele*.

"Ready, then?" the captain asked.

Tom took a breath of his own. "Ready," he answered.

The Battle Begins

Tom and Captain Blaine emerged from the hatch unseen.

As soon as he was on deck, Tom took a huge, deep sniff of the fresh sea air. After all those days in the musty hold, it smelled wonderful! The breeze on his face reminded him instantly of days at home when he ran down to the harbor to see which ships were in. For a moment, he felt so homesick he thought he might cry.

But this was no time for tears. The battle was on!

The pirate ship had drawn up close to the *Adele*, and the pirates had thrown grappling hooks, like giant iron fishhooks, into the *Adele*'s rigging. Then they had swung aboard to take over the ship.

In the weak light of the half-moon that shone above, Tom could make out pirates and sailors wrestling hand to hand all over the deck. Even though he didn't recognize many of the men, it was easy for Tom to tell the pirates from the crew. He spotted the white shirts and blue trousers he'd seen when he first boarded the ship; the men who wore those were the *Adele*'s crew members. The pirates, on the other hand, were dressed in filthy rags with tattered edges, and grimy, worn boots. Their hair was wild and their beards untrimmed. Some of them wore scarves around their heads, and Tom saw the glint of gold in several ears.

A quick glance told Tom that only a few of the pirates were armed; knowing of Ridley's deal, they must have been counting on an easy boarding and surrender. Still, the sight of the pirates sent shivers through his body, and he nearly yelled out loud when Blaine gave him a nudge and pointed out the pirate ship. Its name, painted on the side in red letters, was *Revenge*. Flying from the mast was a tattered Jolly Roger, a horribly grinning white skull on a black background.

Captain Blaine headed for the foredeck, picking his way unnoticed through the tangle of fighting men. From there, according to their plan, the captain would do his best to muster the crew.

Tom's job? Fetch the weapons. He tiptoed to the bow, where Captain Blaine had told him the weapons would be piled. Sure enough, there they lay, shining in the moonlight. Tom shuddered when he saw the fearsome tangle of muskets, pistols, cutlasses, and swords. This battle could become very bloody very soon.

Tom grabbed as many of the weapons as he could and threw a tarp over the rest. Then he headed to the foredeck, weaving his way around the fighting men. Between the darkness of the night and the fact that they were so focused on their fighting, nobody seemed to see him. Tom's heart was beating fast as he scampered back for another load.

He spotted a small pistol and slipped it into his waistband. True, he was only a boy. But shouldn't he be armed, if other men on board had weapons?

Then he heard the sound of a shot. He whirled just in time to see one of the *Adele*'s crew members fall, almost as if in slow motion, over the side of the ship and down into the choppy waves below. A splotch of red spread across his white shirt as he fell, arms cast out wide.

Tom was horrified. He had never seen anything like it in his life! A man had been shot right in front of his eyes. Instantly, Tom knew he could never shoot anyone, pirate or not. He took the pistol out of his waistband and threw it back onto the pile. Looking around wildly, he grabbed a mop that was leaning against the rail. If he was forced to defend himself, at least he would have *something* in his hands.

Tom struggled back to the foredeck, a tangle of weapons in his arms. But where was Captain Blaine? Tom looked around wildly. Had he been captured by the pirates — or thrown overboard by his own men?

Then Tom spotted Blaine, standing still as a statue near the main mast. It had been only minutes since they had come up from below, yet to Tom it seemed like hours.

The captain seemed to be frozen in place.

The pirates were working their way up the deck.

"Now!" Tom urged the captain. "Now or never!"

Captain Blaine looked uncertain.

"Do you want to lose the *Adele*?" Tom asked.

Captain Blaine's lips tightened, and his eyes grew steely. He put his hands on his hips. "All hands on deck!" he bellowed. Then he pulled a whistle out of his pocket and blew a shrill blast. "Assemble on the foredeck!"

Captain Blaine took up a position, keeping the pile of weapons safely behind him. He began shouting out orders, and — miracle of miracles — most of the crew left off fighting (or hiding from pirates!) and came running. The men had been well trained. When they heard a command, they obeyed it without thinking. They lined up in a neat row, awaiting their next order.

"I plan to defend the *Adele* to the death!" roared Captain Blaine. "Are you with me? Yea or nay!"

"Yea!" shouted the men. They stood up straighter.

"Arm the crew," Captain Blaine ordered.

Tom passed out the weapons, then stood back, gripping the mop so tightly that his knuckles stood out, white and bony in the moonlight.

"And now, to battle!"

With Captain Blaine fighting beside them, the men charged the pirates and the true battle began. Tom watched, breathless, as cutlasses swung through the air and shots rang out. A pirate climbed to the top of the rigging, grabbed a rope, and swung feetfirst into the knot of fighting sailors, knocking three men to the deck. One of Blaine's men ran forward and cut the rope with his sword, dumping the pirate into the dark sea below.

Tom stood stock-still. What could he do? How could he help? He had no training in warfare. He was just a boy! He gripped the mop even harder as he watched the men fight.

"Watch out!" yelled Captain Blaine. Tom looked up to see a barrel rolling toward him. In another moment, it would crash into him and send him flying off the deck, down into the cold, dark water. Just in time, Tom leaped to his feet and jumped nimbly over the barrel.

He landed hard and twisted his ankle, but he ignored the shooting pain. All at once, Tom knew what he had to do. He had to protect Blaine — and the *Adele*. He ran toward the fighting men, swinging his mop at every pirate within reach.

Captain Blaine was everywhere, shouting orders, picking up fallen crew members, praising a good shot or a well-landed swing of the cutlass.

Tom watched with admiration. Captain Blaine was a true leader.

As Tom looked on, a pirate charged toward Captain Blaine with his pistol drawn and his finger on the trigger.

Captain Blaine had his back turned. He grunted with effort as he swung his sword at a pirate who was charging from the other direction. He had no idea that he was about to be shot.

"No!" shouted Tom.

■ ■ ■

"No!" shouted Leo. Mr. Taylor made the story sound so real that Leo could practically *see* the pirate charging at Captain Blaine. No matter

how strict the captain had been, he didn't deserve to be murdered in cold blood.

Mr. Taylor stopped and looked down at Leo. "Should I stop?" he asked.

Leo glanced at the clock. There were only a few minutes left before the last bell rang. He just *had* to hear how the story came out. "No way!" he said. "What happened next?"

Victory

Tom dashed forward, swinging the mop with all his strength. He caught the pistol-aiming pirate in the knees and threw him off balance. The scoundrel fell to his knees and his pistol slid, clattering along the deck. Tom grabbed it and threw it overboard before the pirate could struggle to his feet.

Blaine whirled just in time to see what had happened. He grinned at Tom. "I owe you one!" he said. Then he turned back toward his other attacker, swinging his sword.

The fight seemed to go on for ages. Tom lost count of how many men had gone overboard and how many lay groaning on the deck. But before long, it became clear that Blaine's men were winning the battle.

"O'Hara!" shouted Blaine at a man with a long

braided beard and a dragon tattoo down his arm. "Surrender now if you want to survive!"

The pirate captain grimaced. But he knew the battle was over. The pirates had been taken by surprise. They had expected a distracted, disorganized crew, ripe for the picking. Instead, they were facing a finely trained fighting machine.

O'Hara stood looking back at Blaine, a stubborn frown on his face. But after a few moments, the pirate threw down his cutlass. "That's it, lads!" O'Hara shouted to his ragtag crew. "We've been beat."

When the pirates were all tied up and the *Adele* was made shipshape once more, Captain Blaine set a course for Charleston, towing the pirate ship *Revenge* behind the *Adele*. When they reached port, he sent word to the local authorities. The sheriff and his men hauled the blackguards — including Mister Ridley — off the ship.

After that, Blaine arranged to restock the ship with food and water. They were setting sail again for Barbados, and there was no time to waste. This time, Tom noticed, Captain Blaine didn't just stand

and watch while the men loaded the ship. He didn't shout orders or urge them to hurry up. Instead, he joined them, hauling crates and barrels up the gangplank. He laughed and joked with the crew. And that night he held a feast to end all feasts, to celebrate the *Adele*'s victory over the pirates. It was the first real meal Tom had eaten since that Sunday dinner at home, and he ate until he nearly keeled over.

Tom had a feeling that Captain Blaine was going to be a different kind of captain from now on. Of course, he would still drill his men and make sure they were ready for anything. But neither he nor his crew would ever forget the victory they had claimed while fighting side by side on the decks of the *Adele*. Now the men had a leader they could respect and admire. There would never again be talk of mutiny aboard that ship.

Captain Blaine did one more thing before setting sail.

He sent a telegraph to Tom's mother. ■ ■ ■

"Oh, man! So he had to go home?" Leo asked. "After he'd saved the ship and the crew and everything?"

"Go home?" asked Mr. Taylor. "Oh, no. Captain Blaine just wanted to make sure that Tom's mother didn't worry. He knew Tom had earned that trip to Barbados. And just like him, the boy who had started out a stowaway would spend most of his life at sea." He nodded and leaned back to finish the story.

■ ■ ■

The Adele *left Charleston on a bright, sparkling day, sailing south.* Tom, dressed in navy blue trousers and a white shirt, climbed up high in the rigging. He looked back as the land receded. When he couldn't make out even a trace of the harbor they'd visited, Tom turned forward and faced into the wind. He could almost smell the tropical breezes of Barbados.

Tom went back home after that trip, his arms loaded with carved coconuts and lengths of bright woven cloth to give as gifts to family and friends.

But as soon as he was old enough he signed on to a ship and rarely slept on land again, just like Captain Blaine. He never forgot one moment of his first days aboard the *Adele*, not even when he was captain of his own ship, twenty years later. And he always made sure there was a cat aboard, preferably a gray one with six toes on every paw.

The End

Cricket started clapping when Mr. Taylor finished, and everybody else joined in. Everybody but Leo. He was just smiling and shaking his head.

"All right, all right, I get it," Leo said to Mr. Taylor. "You've talked me into it. I'll stick with soccer."

"Soccer?" asked Mr. Taylor, raising an eyebrow. "What does soccer have to do with Tom's story?"

"It has everything to do with it," said Leo. "I mean, that was a great story and all, but basically it's about how doing drills can come in handy. Like the way Captain Blaine could pull his men together to fight the pirates, because of the way they'd been trained." He gave Mr. Taylor a challenging look.

"Hmm." Mr. Taylor met his gaze unblinkingly. "I hadn't thought of that. I really just remembered that story because of the mop." He waved a hand at the corner where the mop was leaning.

"The mop?" Cricket asked. She jumped up and ran to grab it. "Is there something special about this —" She stared down at the wooden handle. "Oh, wow!" she said breathlessly.

"What?" Jennifer asked.

Cricket brought the mop back to the reading corner and passed it to Leo. He looked down at the handle.

There were words burned into the wood. Leo looked at them, amazed. He couldn't believe his eyes.

"PROPERTY OF THE *Adele*," the dark letters read.

Jason grabbed it to see what Leo was looking at. "Where did you *get* that?" he demanded.

"From a friend," was all Mr. Taylor said. He smiled mysteriously.

"But — I thought the story was all made up," Leo said.

Mr. Taylor smiled. "You asked for a story that could really happen," he answered, "didn't you?"

"Yes, but —"

"What Leo means is, how did you get all his things in there, like the cat and the pirate ship and the cheese?" asked Oliver very seriously, pushing up his glasses.

"And the key," Jennifer reminded him. "Don't forget about the key."

"I didn't *get* them in," said Mr. Taylor. "They're just part of the story." He stretched out his long arms. Then he reached up to turn off the lamp just as the last bell rang.

Mr. Taylor went to his desk and picked up his red *Taylor-Made Tales* notebook. Leo figured he was going to take it home and add the latest story. Leo's story. He didn't know quite how Mr. Taylor had done it. How could all those things turn up in the story? Was it magic? Or just coincidence? Leo didn't care. The important thing was that now Leo's story would be in the book forever.

■ ■ ■

Leo was thinking hard as he pulled his soccer bag out of his cubby. He had already pretty much decided what he was going to say to Coach Hauser at practice. "Thanks for asking me to be your assistant coach," he'd say. "But I've decided I really want to play."

When he got to the corner, Leo saw Pete waiting for him. Pete raised an eyebrow. "Well?" he asked.

"Well, well, well," said Leo. "Three holes in the ground." It was one of his favorite jokes — which meant that Pete had heard it too many times to still laugh at it.

"Come on, Leo," Pete said. "You know what I mean. Are you quitting, or not?"

"You'll find out," Leo said. "Race you to the field!" He took off running, his soccer bag bumping against his legs in that old familiar way.

When they got to the field, Coach Hauser was waiting. But this time his arms weren't crossed, and he didn't look mad. "All right, Leo!" he yelled when he saw them racing toward the home bench. He pretended to drop a finish-line flag. "And the winner is — Leo Murray, by a nose! Or an elbow. Or something."

Leo threw down his bag. "Coach," he began, but Coach Hauser held up a hand to stop him.

"Leo," he said, "I've been thinking about it. Your ideas were great, but I realized I need you more as a player than as a coach. What do you say?"

"I say — yeah!" Leo shouted. Suddenly, he couldn't wait to play. He knew they'd have to run laps first and then do some drills, but at least they'd probably have some time to scrimmage, too.

But Coach surprised Leo and the rest of the Piranhas. "No laps today," he said. "You guys are all in great shape. Laps are boring. I want to start with something fun, instead." He held up a sheaf of papers. "I talked to a few coaching friends and got some great new ideas. We can work on our skills and have a good time, too."

Coach had them partner up, and he paired each set of partners with a set of opponents. Then he pointed to two rows of cones he had set up in a random obstacle course. "Those are coral reefs," he said. "One team has just had to walk the plank, and now you're swimming for your life. The other players are your opponents. They are sharks. If you and your partner can dribble and pass the ball through the reef and all the way to the goal without the sharks stealing it, you win."

Everybody cheered and ran onto the field.

Leo kicked a ball to Pete. "Yahoo!" He was back in action. Not only that, it looked like practice was going to be a lot more fun from now on.

"Great drill!" he yelled to Coach Hauser. "What's it called?"

Coach smiled. "Pirates!" he said.

About the Author

Ellen Miles has always loved a good story. She also loves biking, skiing, writing, and playing with her dog, Django. Django is a black Lab who would rather eat a book than read one.

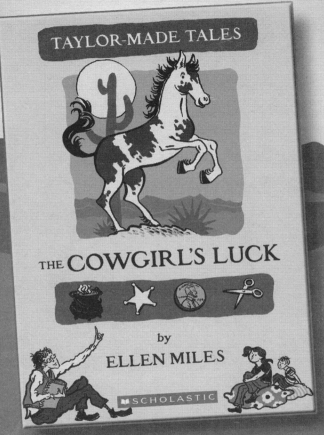

Thrilling tales of adventure and danger...

Emily Rodda's

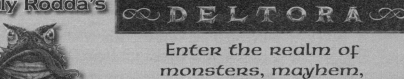

DELTORA

Enter the realm of
monsters, mayhem,
and magic of Deltora Quest,
Deltora Shadowlands, and
Dragons of Deltora

Gordon Korman's

ON THE RUN

The chase is on in this heart-stopping series about two
fugitive kids who must follow a trail of clues to prove
their parents' innocence.

Gregor the Overlander
by Suzanne Collins

In the Underland, Gregor must face giant talking
cockroaches, rideable bats, and a legendary
Rat King to save his family, himself, and
maybe the entire subterranean world.

Available wherever you buy books.

MORE SERIES YOU'LL LOVE

Abracadabra!

The members of the Abracadabra Club have a few tricks up their sleeves—and a few tricks you can learn to do yourself!

A JIGSAW JONES MYSTERY

Jigsaw and his partner, Mila, know that mysteries are like jigsaw puzzles— you've got to look at all the pieces to solve the case!

THE SECRETS OF DROON
by TONY ABBOTT

Time for a magic carpet ride! Join Eric, Julie, and Neal on their wild adventures as they help Princess Keeah save the secret, magical world of Droon.

www.scholastic.com/kids

LITTLE APPLE

■ SCHOLASTIC

FILLLA8